This book belongs to:

Jenaya

Here's my fingerprint
to prove it:

STERLING CHILDREN'S BOOKS
New York

Dip your fingers into white paint and
give this mouth some pearly teeth!

Make some bold splashes
to show a storm on the sea.

Finish the underwater world and use fingerprints to show who lives in the deep sea.

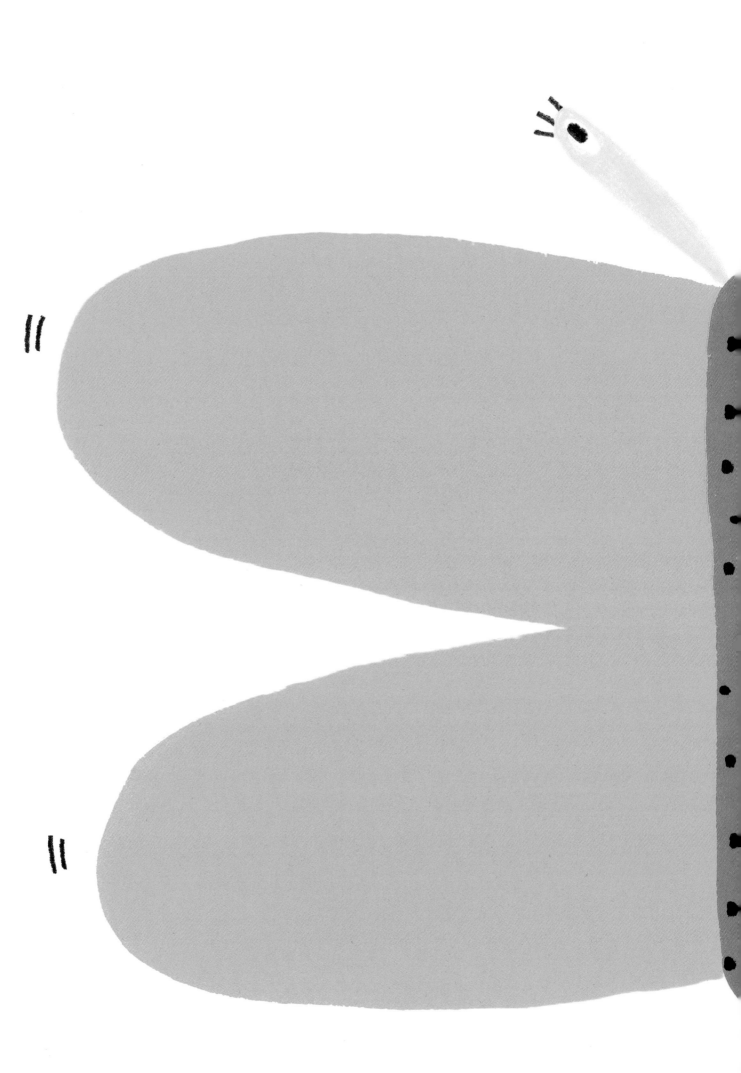

Paint one side of the butterfly,
using spots, splashes, and fingerprints.
Then, while the paint is wet, tightly
close the book and open it again!

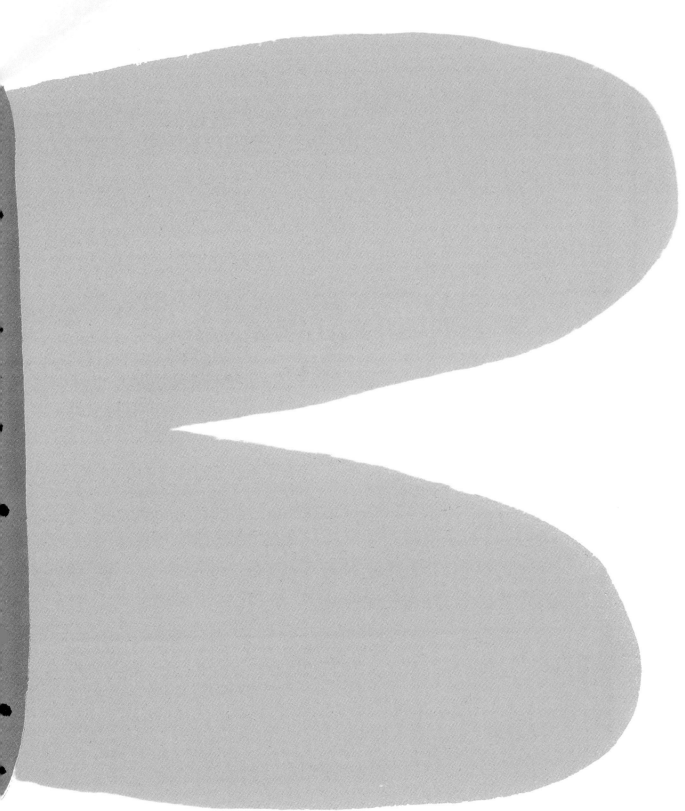

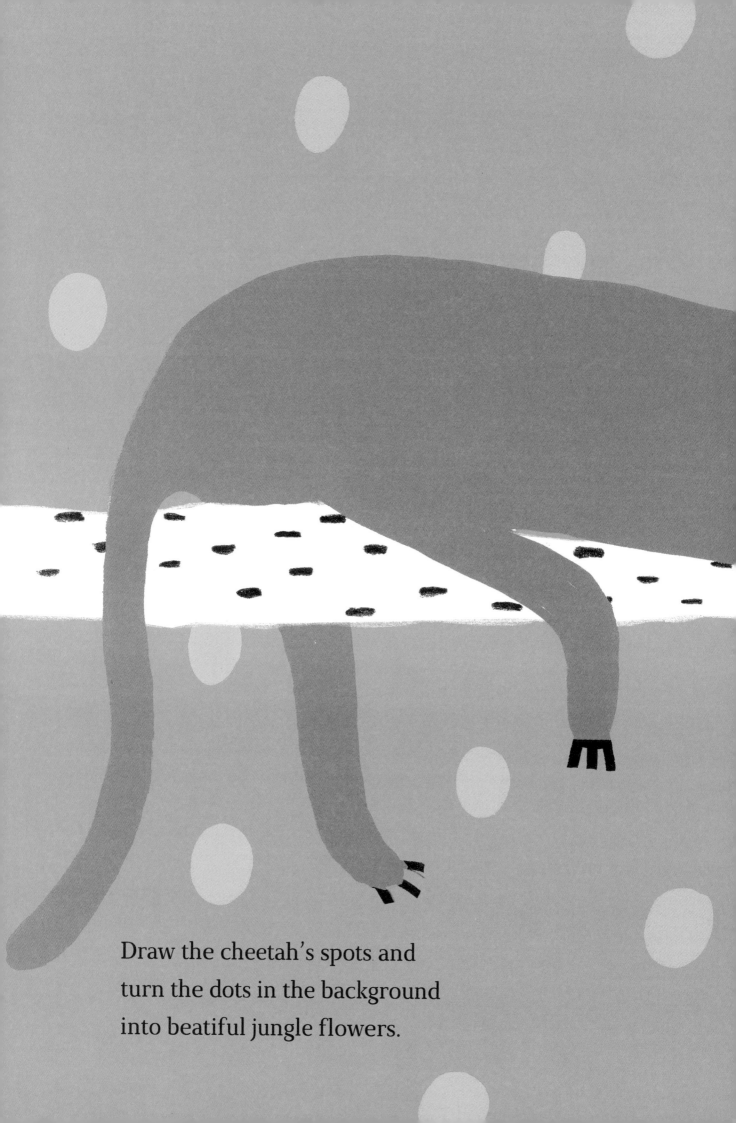

Draw the cheetah's spots and
turn the dots in the background
into beatiful jungle flowers.

What can you turn this big spot into?

Stamp a loved one's fingerprints inside
this frame. Then, decorate the frame.

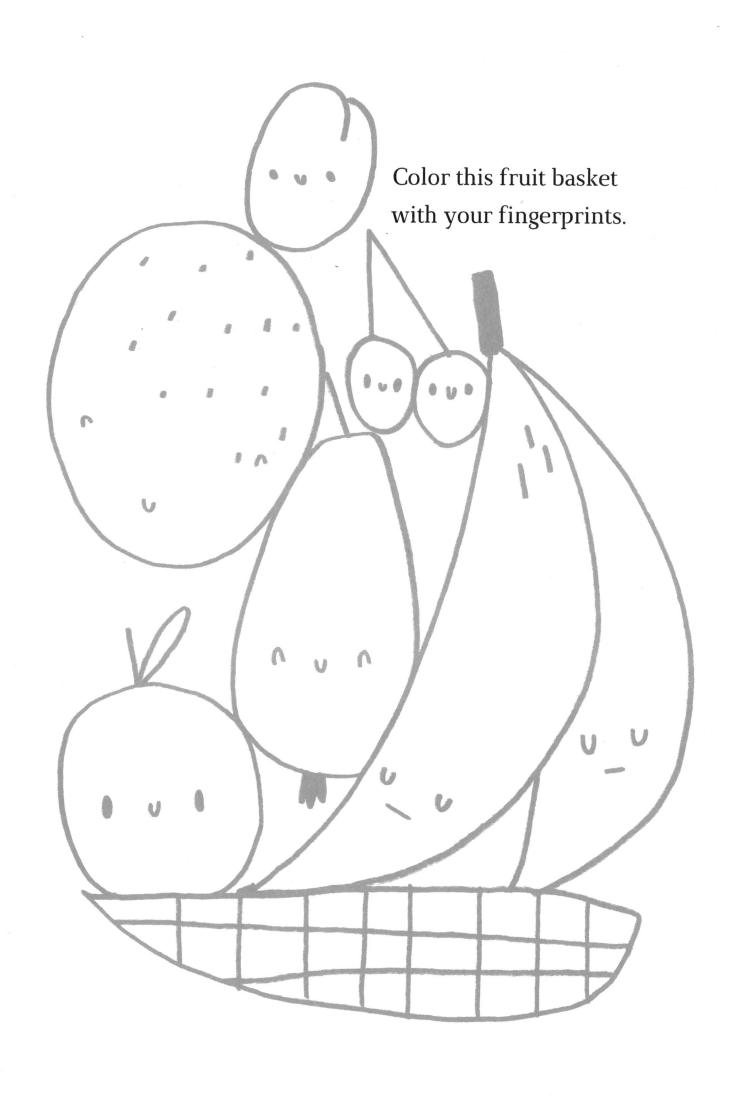

Color this fruit basket
with your fingerprints.

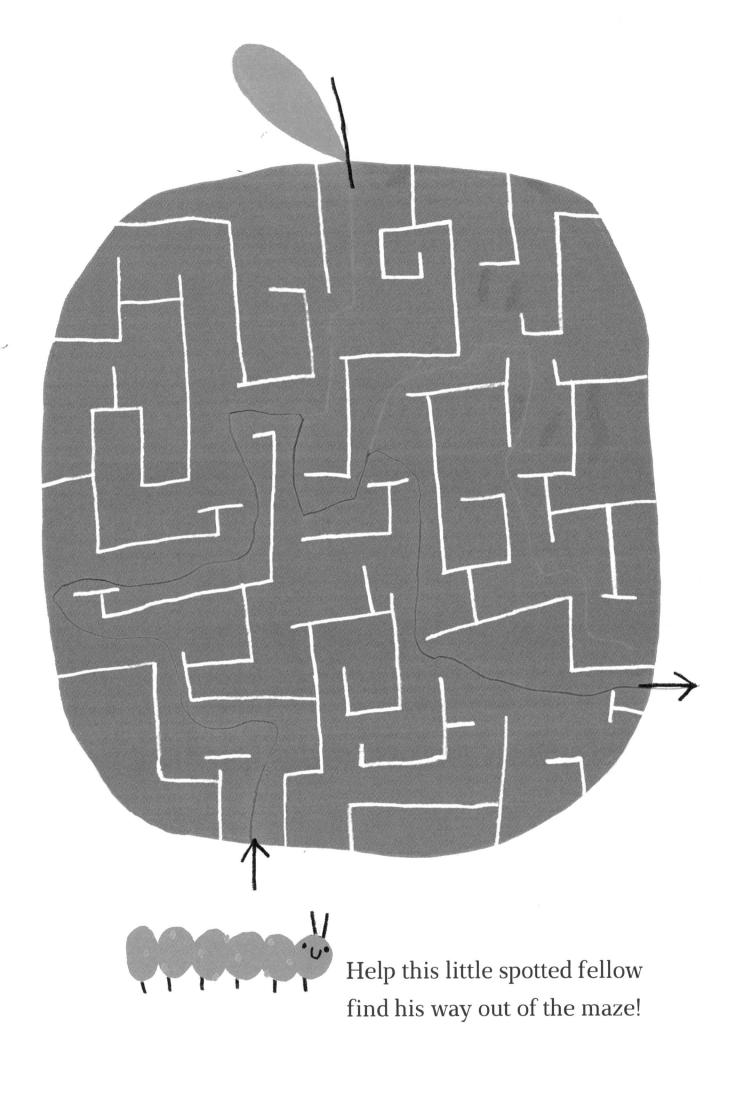

Help this little spotted fellow
find his way out of the maze!

Where are the ice cream scoops?
Use your fingerprints to make
your favorite ice cream flavors.

Decorate these pillows with patterns
made of splashes and spots!

What is this going to be? Rain?
A blue beehive? Finish the picture.

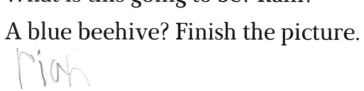

A   B   C   D   E

F   G   H   I   J

K   L   M   N   O

P   Q   R   S   T

U   V   W   X   Y

Make your own code using different spots.
Then use it to write a message to a friend.

Z

It's time for apple picking!
Use your fingerprints to give these
trees lots of leaves and more apples!

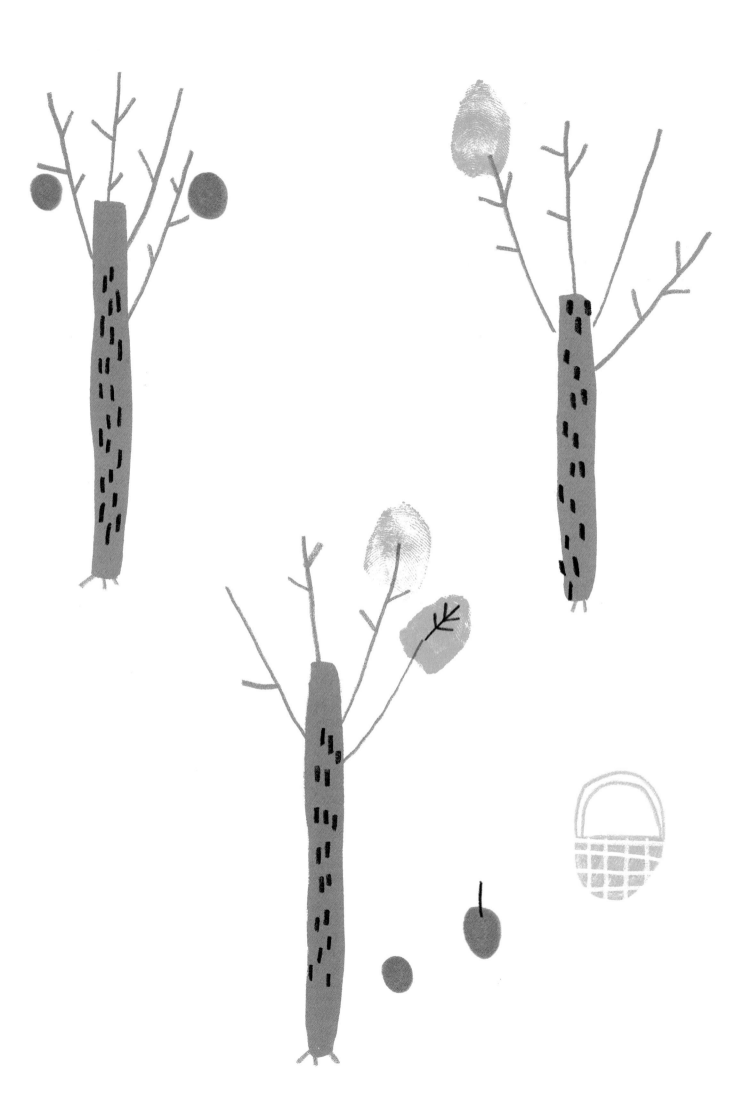

Use white paint and fingerprints
to finish this winter wonderland.

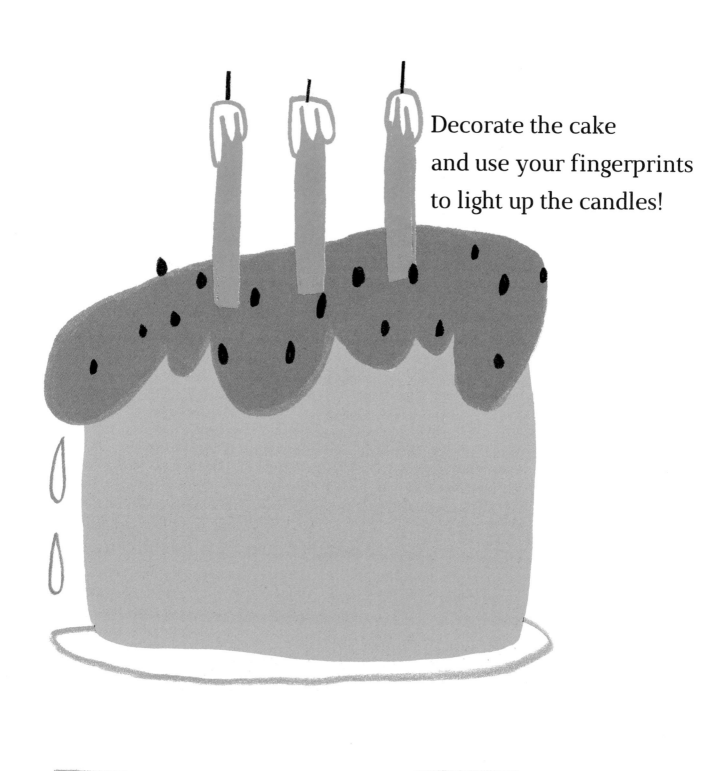

Decorate the cake
and use your fingerprints
to light up the candles!

Splash paint to show the volcano erupting!

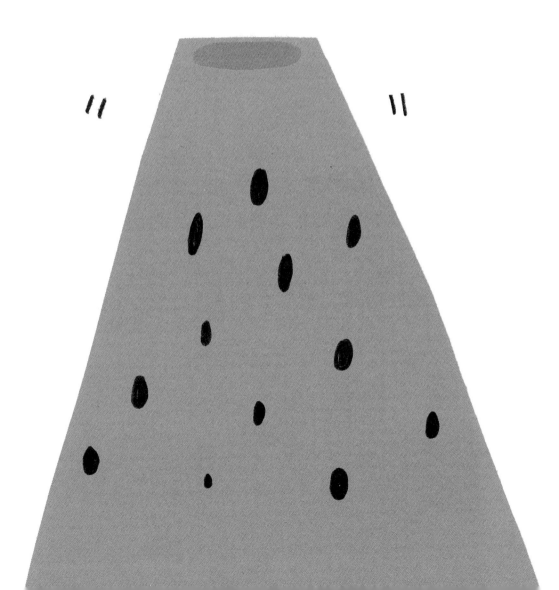

The rain is coming!
Make some rainy clouds
with your fingerprints
and hide the sun.

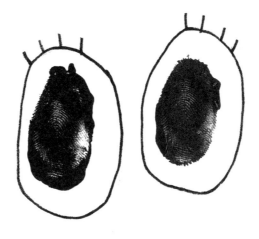

Finish this picture.

Whose eyes are these?

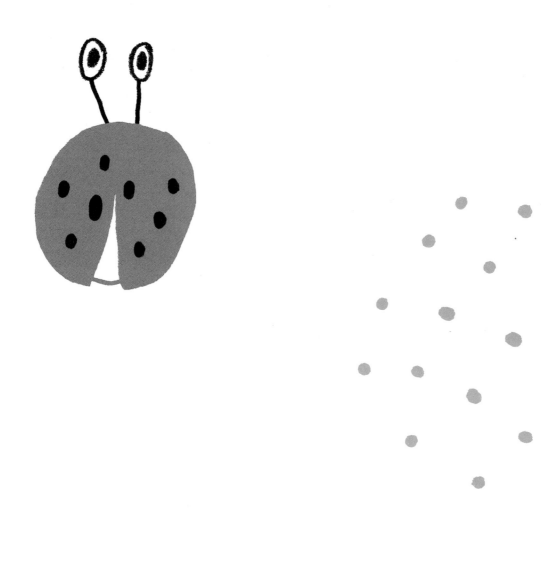

What creatures
could these spots
belong to?

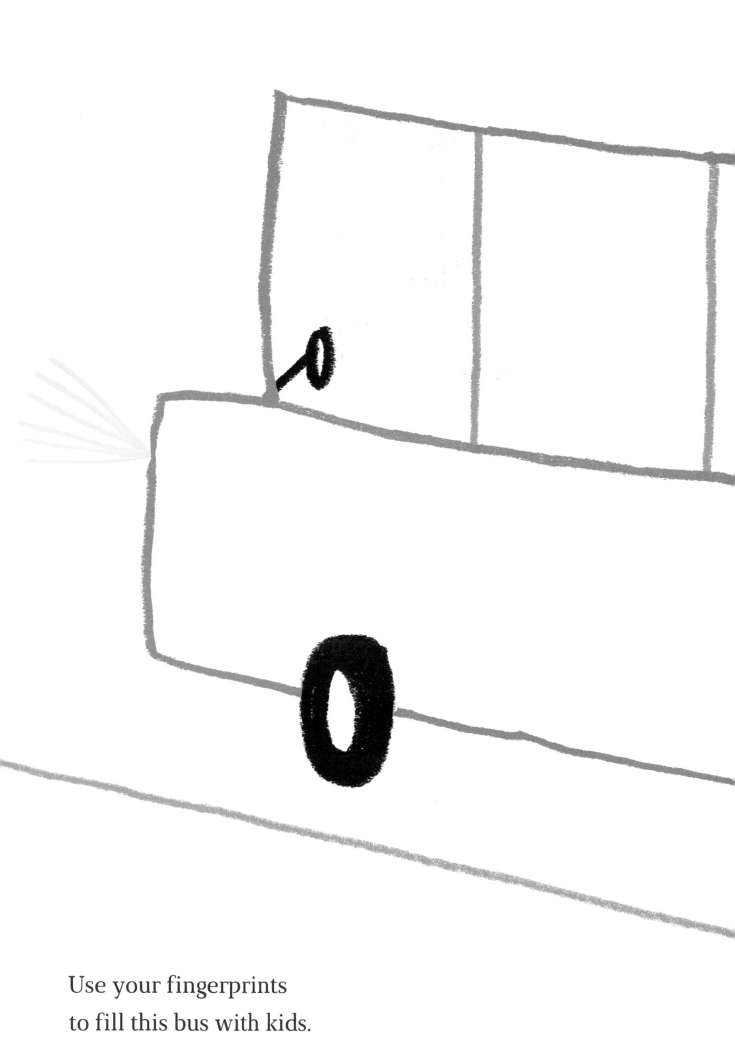

Use your fingerprints
to fill this bus with kids.

Splash some paint and make more fireworks!

YAY!

Use your fingerprints
and give this poodle
a nice hairdo!

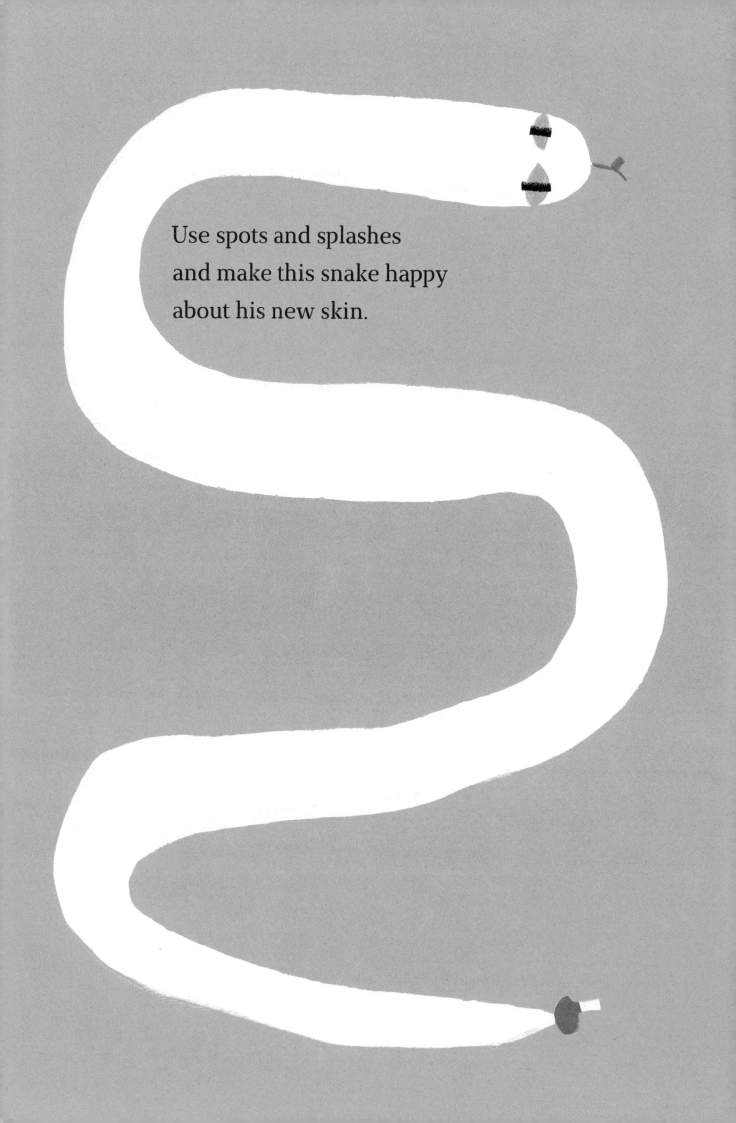

Use spots and splashes
and make this snake happy
about his new skin.

Finish this comic strip! What will this story be about?

See these spots?
They're actually the buttons
of a super-secret time machine.
Draw the machine!

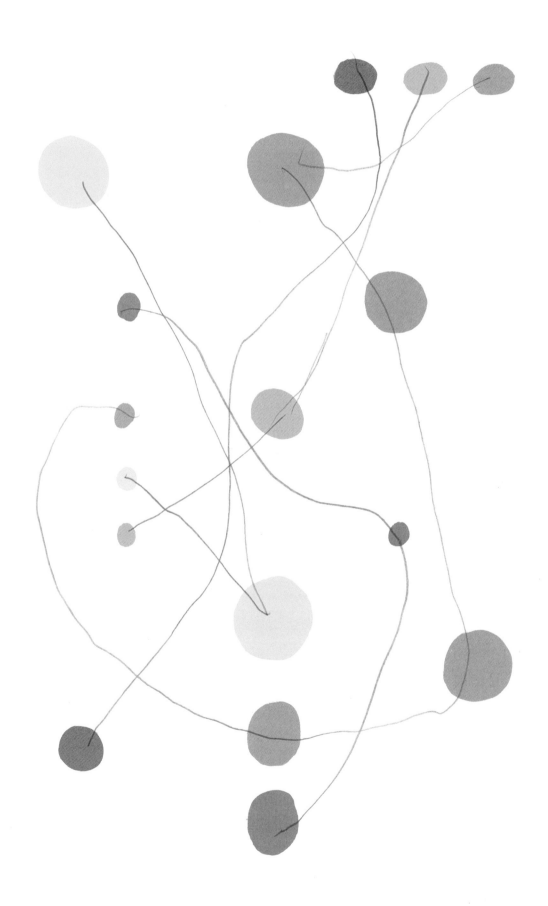

Welcome to space! Color these planets and name them. Will they have rings like Saturn or giant craters? Add some splashes to make a meteor shower.

This little rascal stepped into a bucket of paint!
Use spots to show how he gets out of the maze.

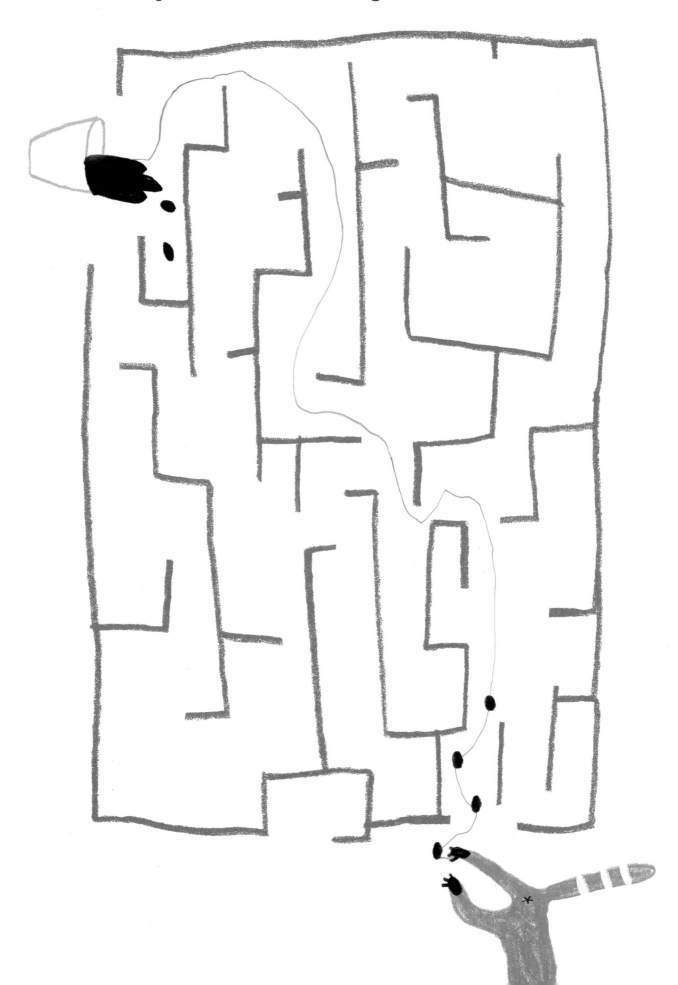

Follow the lines
and see who will get
the chocolate chip cookie!

Who and what can we find
living deep in the grass?

Turn these spots
into wheels and draw
cars racing on the track!

It's bath time! Use white paint splashes to show the water running and fingerprints to make soap foam. Don't forget to draw who's taking a bath!

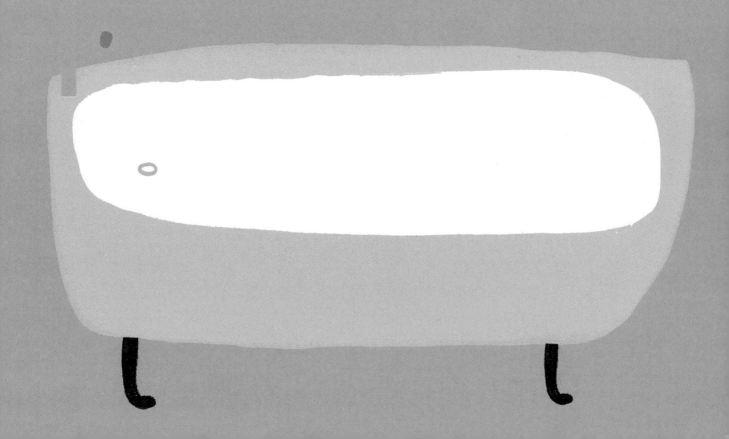

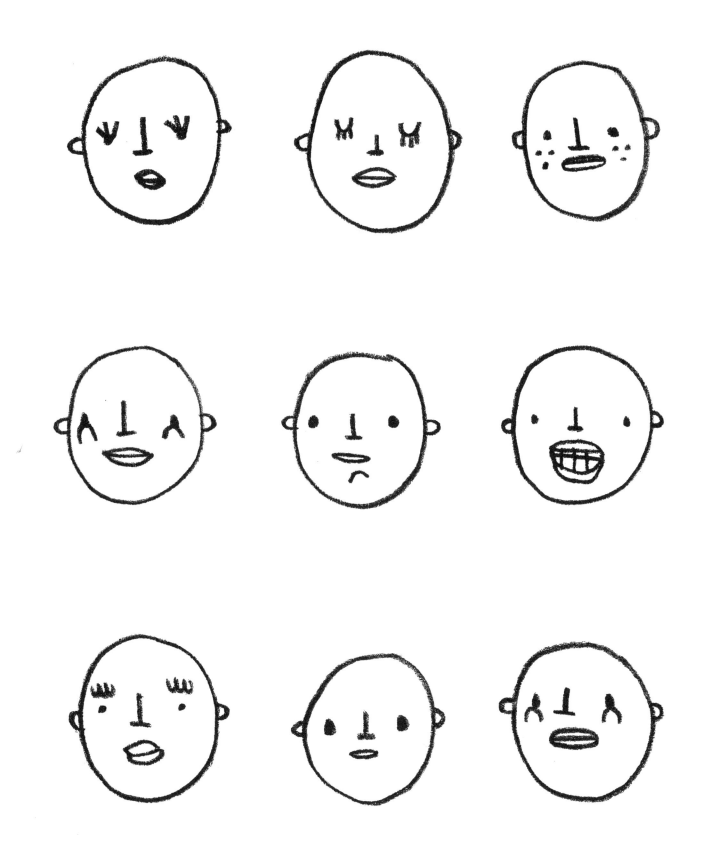

Make some crazy hairstyles with paint splashes.

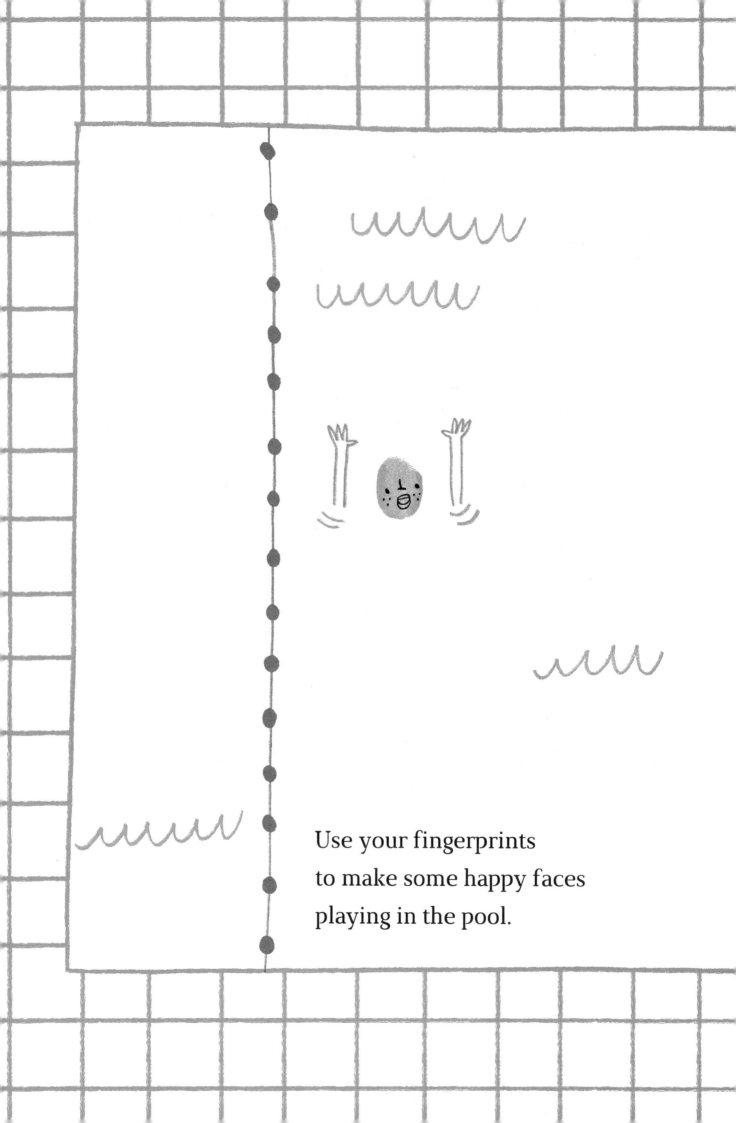

Use your fingerprints
to make some happy faces
playing in the pool.

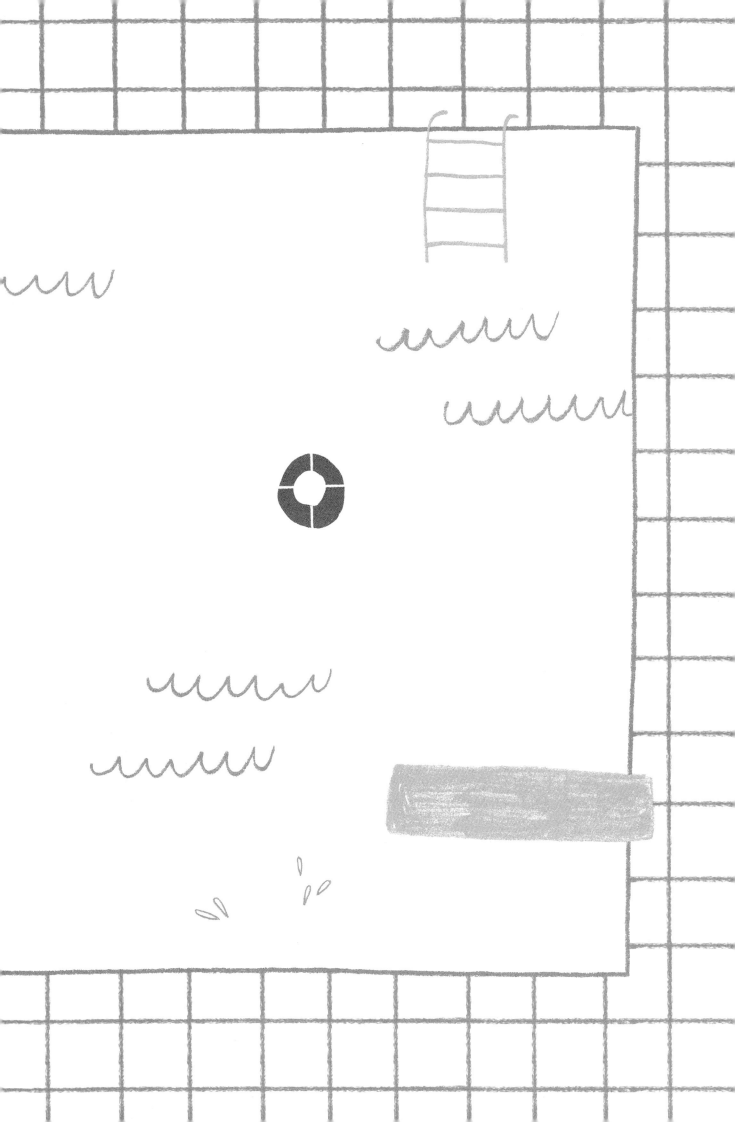

What kinds of birds can you
make with fingerprints?

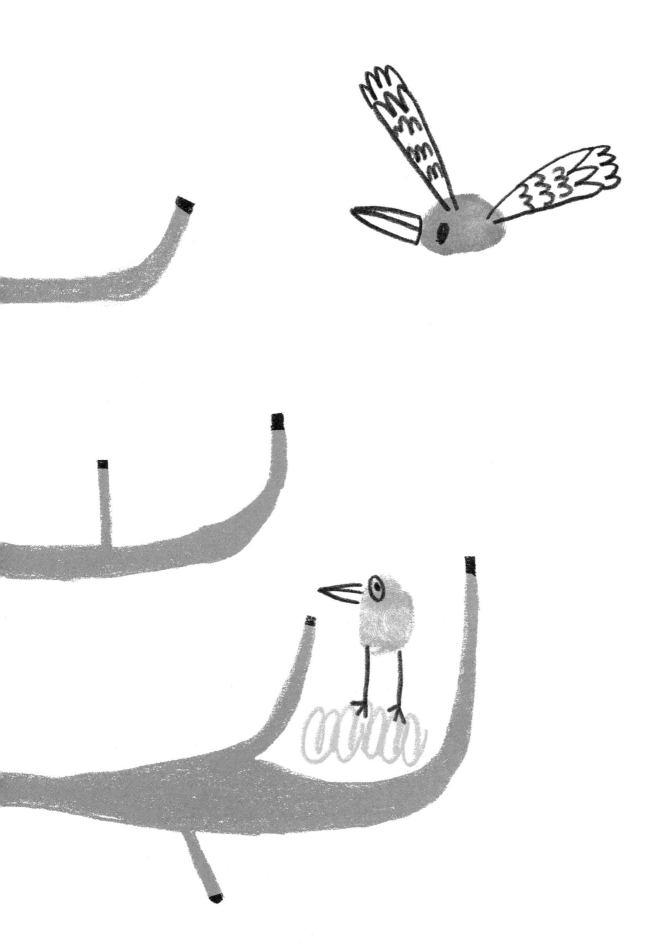

Each of these blank spots
is a place to write a secret!
Paint them black when you
finish writing so your
secrets are safe!

Make a fingerprint
pattern for this
lady's lovely dress.

Color the picture and make as many holes as you can in this block of cheese.

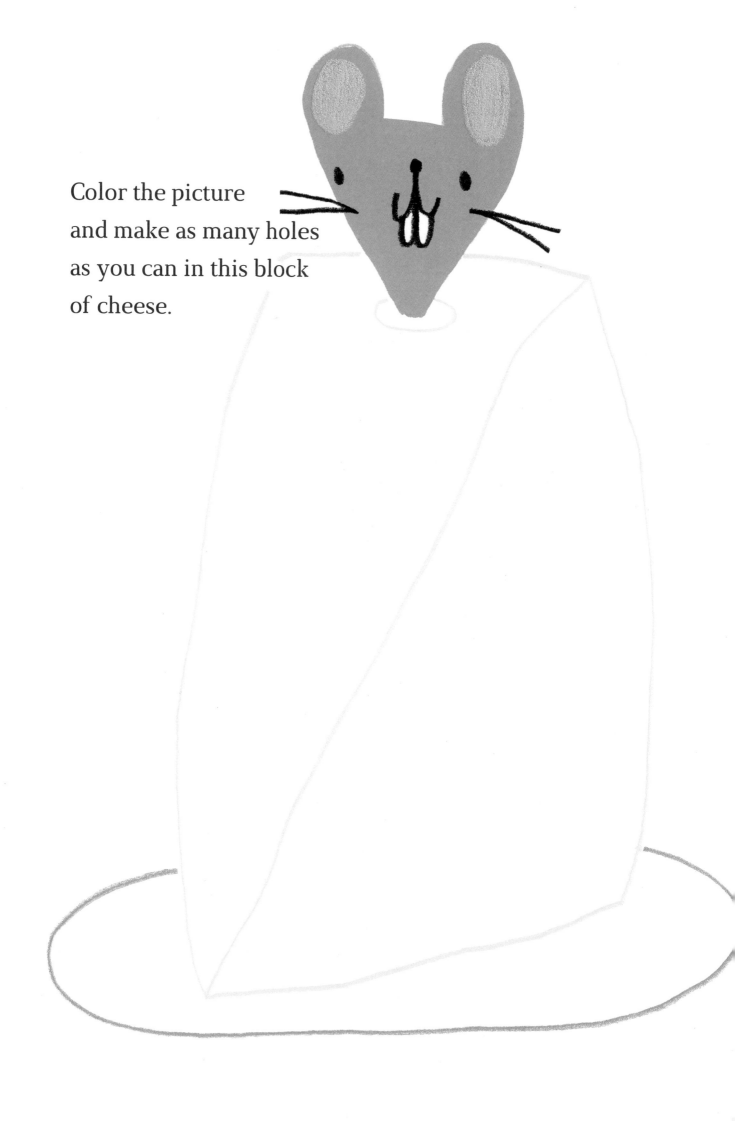

Connect the dots.

Set the table and make food out of fingerprints.

STERLING CHILDREN'S BOOKS
New York

An Imprint of Sterling Publishing
1166 Avenue of the Americas
New York, NY 10036

First Sterling edition published in 2018.

ISBN 978-1-4549-2931-4

Distributed in Canada by Sterling Publishing
c/o Canadian Manda Group, 664 Annette Street - Toronto, Ontario, M6S 2C8, Canada

For information about custom editions, special sales, and premium and corporate purchases,
please contact Sterling Special Sales at 800-805-5489 or specialsales@sterlingpublishing.com.

Manufactured in China
Lot #:
2 4 6 8 10 9 7 5 3 1
12/17

sterlingpublishing.com

TOP SECRET